OCTONAUTS

and the Decorator Crab

The daring crew of the Octopod are ready to embark on an exciting new mission!

INKLING OCTOPUS
(Professor)

KWAZII CAT
(Lieutenant)

PESO PENGUIN
(Medic)

BARNACLES BEAR
(Captain)

TWEAK BUNNY
(Engineer)

SHELLINGTON SEA OTTER
(Field Researcher)

DASHI DOG
(Photographer)

TUNIP THE VEGIMAL
(Ship's Cook)

EXPLORE . RESCUE . PROTECT

OCTONAUTS

and the Decorator Crab

SIMON AND SCHUSTER

"Yeow!"

Kwazii was playing with a ball of wool, when it bounced out of his quarters...

all the way

down to the

launch bay.

"Got it!"
Captain Barnacles tossed the ball back to Kwazii, then pointed up at the radar screen.
"Something's heading straight for us, Cap'!" gulped Tweak.

The Octonauts braced themselves for a nasty bump.
The dot on the radar screen got closer and closer until…
nothing happened!

Suddenly the radar screen went blank.
"Kwazii!" said Barnacles. **"Sound the Octoalert!"**

"Octonauts, to

Tweak, Barnacles and Kwazii swam out to investigate the broken radar.

"The radar dish isn't broken," frowned Tweak. "It's gone!"

"A scurvy thief is around here somewhere," growled Kwazii. "I'll find him with my spyglass."

Splat! Before he could spot the crook, a clump of seaweed squelched across the lens.

"Use my binoculars instead," said Barnacles. "Tweak and I will search the other side of the Octopod."

Kwazii squinted through the binoculars.
Apart from a few floating fish, the ocean was empty.

"Yeow!"
The spyglass was gone – swiped
from under Kwazii's whiskers.
The thief had struck again!

🐙 FACT: RADAR DISH

A radar dish can detect animals moving outside the Octopod.

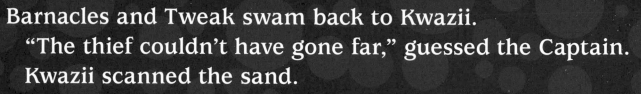

Barnacles and Tweak swam back to Kwazii.

"The thief couldn't have gone far," guessed the Captain.
Kwazii scanned the sand.

"Aha!" he whispered. "A trail!"

A bumpy line of tracks curved along
the seabed, but it quickly disappeared.

"This thief is sneaky,"
declared Barnacles. "So we'll
just have to be sneakier.
Return to the launch bay!"

As soon as they got back to the Octopod, Tweak started work on the GUP-A. The sub was mission-ready in five minutes flat!

"Push that button, Captain," said Tweak.

Barnacles pressed a yellow button on the control board. Seaweed green stripes flashed all over the gup's metalwork.

"Camouflage!" grinned the Captain. "Now no one will see us."

Barnacles, Kwazii and Peso climbed into the GUP-A. "Open the Octohatch!"

The GUP-A darted up and
down the reef, scouring
the ocean for clues.
"**Woah!**" cried Kwazii.
"That plant just took a walk!"

The crew peered out of the
porthole – the seaweed really was moving!
"Follow that plant!" bellowed Kwazii. "He's got my
spyglass!"
"Octonauts, let's investigate," said Barnacles.

The crew activated their diving helmets, then dropped through the gup's exit hatch.

"You need help!" said Peso, spotting a purple anemone with a sore tentacle.

The clever medic soon had the anemone feeling better. But when he packed up his medical bag, his bandages had disappeared!

"The thief strikes again!" yelped Kwazii.

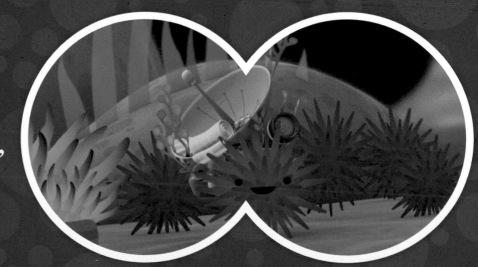

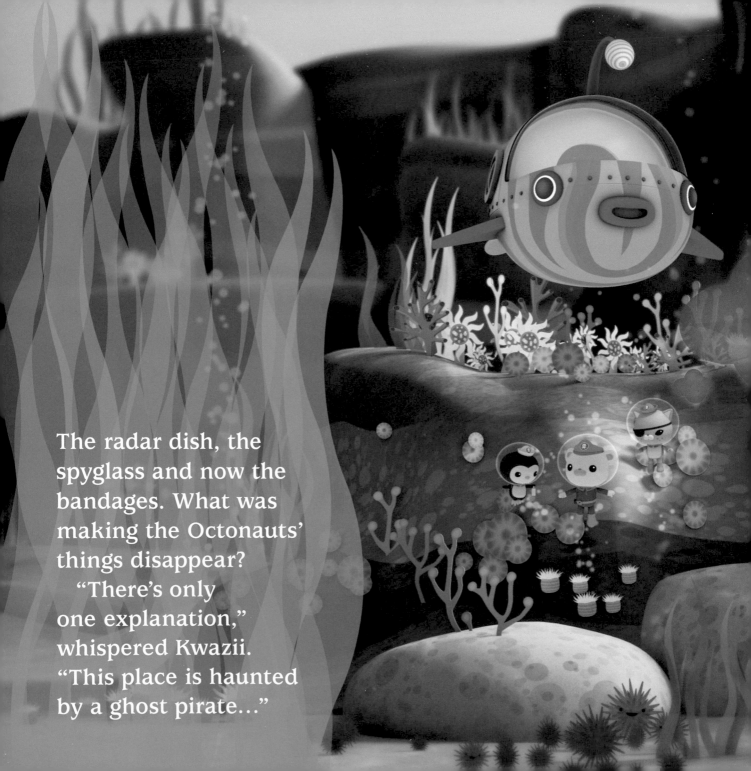

The radar dish, the spyglass and now the bandages. What was making the Octonauts' things disappear?

"There's only one explanation," whispered Kwazii. "This place is haunted by a ghost pirate..."

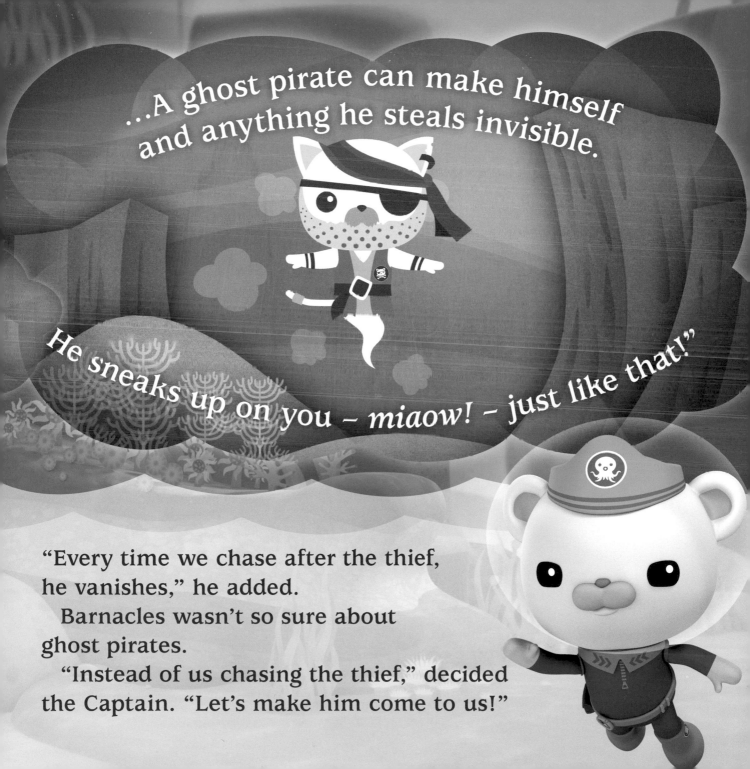

...A ghost pirate can make himself and anything he steals invisible.

He sneaks up on you – *miaow!* – just like that!"

"Every time we chase after the thief, he vanishes," he added.

Barnacles wasn't so sure about ghost pirates.

"Instead of us chasing the thief," decided the Captain. "Let's make him come to us!"

The plan was simple.

"We'll throw this ball of wool out for the thief to steal," explained Barnacles. "When he comes near us, the GUP-A's alarm will sound and then…"

"We'll get him!" yelled Kwazii.

Barnacles nodded, turning on the gup's extra camouflage. Now all the Octonauts had to do was **wait…**

…and wait…

…and w-a-i-t…

…and

…and

z-z-z-z-zzzzzzzzz

na-na-na-na-na-na-na-na-na-NA!
The GUP-A's noisy alarm made the Octonauts jump up.
Someone was tugging at its seaweed moustache!

"Don't let him steal it from under our noses!"
cried Barnacles.

The crew swam after the mystery thief. Before you could
say 'shiver me whiskers' the crook was cornered on a rock.

"We've got him!" exclaimed Kwazii.

The creature loaded up with all their equipment was a decorator crab!

"Easy there, fella," said Barnacles. "Just return what you stole and you can be on your way."

"I was only trying to cover my shell," explained the crab, looking very sorry.

When he had handed everything back, Barnacles plucked the moustache off the GUP-A.

"This will keep you camouflaged," he smiled. 'A gift to you from the Octonauts."

As soon as the crew got back to the Octopod, Tweak screwed the stolen dish back in place. The Octonauts cheered in the launch bay when the radar screen lit up again.

"Good work, Tweak!" signalled Barnacles.

"Thanks Cap'!" grinned Tweak. "I did make one other little change out here..."

FACT: CAMOUFLAGE

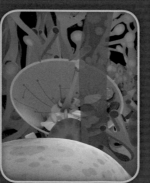

The decorator crab attaches things to its shell so nobody can see it.

A funny green moustache suddenly popped up on the Octopod.

The Octonauts laughed and laughed. Not so far away in a hidden corner of the reef, a little decorator crab chuckled too.

"Calling all Octonauts! Our mission to find those lost objects taught us lots about the decorator crab. What a camouflage expert! Here's my special report showing exactly what we know about this resourceful little creature."

FACT FILE: THE DECORATOR CRAB

The decorator crab covers its shell with anything it can find – sponges, coral, even sea anemones.

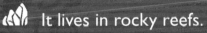 It lives in rocky reefs.

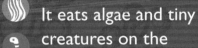 It eats algae and tiny creatures on the sea floor.

OCTOFACTS:

1. The decorator crab camouflages itself to stay safe from predators, especially sharks.

2. The creature looks like a scuttling piece of seaweed.

3. The crab makes a special glue to stick stuff to its shell.

Dive into these thrilling Octonauts books!

and the Whale Shark

and the Decorator Crab

More
great books
splash-landing
soon...

Ready for Action
in the GUP – A!

Meet the Crew

WWW.THEOCTONAUTS.COM

www.simonandschuster.co.uk